The Velveteen Rabbit

D1416209

By Margery Williams
Adapted by Ashley Crownover
Illustrated by Sherry Neidigh

Copyright © 1999 Dalmatian Press, LLC. All rights reserved. 11270
Printed in the U.S.A.
The DALMATIAN PRESS name and logo are trademarks of
Dalmatian Press, LLC, Franklin, Tennessee 37067.
Written permission must be secured from the publisher to use or reproduce any part of this book.

Dalmatian
Press

There was once a beautiful Velveteen Rabbit.
His coat was spotted brown and white, and his ears
were lined with pink satin. On Christmas morning
he was the most wonderful gift in the Boy's stocking.
All morning, the Boy played with him. Then, in the
excitement of looking at all the other
presents, the Velveteen
Rabbit was forgotten.

For a long time nobody paid much attention to the Rabbit. The mechanical toys were rude to him because he was only a stuffed bunny. But the Play Horse, who had been there longer than any of the other toys—and knew all about toy magic— was very kind to the Rabbit.

One day the Rabbit asked the Play Horse, "What is Real? Does it mean having batteries or lights?"

"Real isn't how you are made," said the Play Horse. "It's a thing that happens to you. When a child really loves you, that is when you become Real."

One evening at bedtime, the Boy couldn't find the toy dog that slept with him, so his mother gave him the Rabbit instead. From then on, the Velveteen Rabbit slept with the Boy every night. The Boy would talk to him and they would play wonderful games—in whispers. The Rabbit slept snug and warm in the Boy's arms all night long.

Spring came, and wherever the Boy went, the Rabbit went, too. He had rides in the wheelbarrow and picnics on the grass. One day, he heard the Boy tell his mother, "My Bunny is Real. He's not a stuffed toy."

That was the happiest day of the Rabbit's life.

After a while, the Velveteen Rabbit got raggedy
from being loved so much. Some of his fur rubbed
off and the pink in his ears faded, but the Boy didn't notice.
He thought his Bunny was beautiful. When summer came,
they played together in the woods almost every day.

Then one day, the Boy got very, very sick.
The doctor said that all the toys in the room
had to be tossed out because they were full of
bad germs. The Boy got better, but the little
Rabbit was put in a sack with the other things
and taken outside.

The Velveteen Rabbit wriggled his way to the
top of the sack and looked out. Nearby he could
see the woods where he and the Boy had played.
He thought of how happy those times had been,
and of how much the Boy had loved him.
A tear trickled down his little shabby
nose and fell to the ground.
  Then a strange thing happened...

Where the tear fell, a mysterious flower began to grow.
It had emerald leaves and a beautiful golden blossom.
The blossom opened and a fairy stepped out. "I am the
Toy Magic Fairy," she said. "I take care of the playthings
that children have loved. When they are old and worn out,
I make them Real."

"But wasn't I Real before?" the Rabbit asked.

The fairy said, "You were Real to the Boy because he loved you. Now you shall be Real to everyone."

In the meadow, the Velveteen Rabbit saw wild rabbits dancing with their shadows on the velvet grass.

"Run and play, little Rabbit," said the Toy Magic Fairy. "You are a Real Rabbit now."

Fall and winter passed. In the spring, when the days grew warm and sunny, the Boy went out to play. In the woods he saw two rabbits peeping at him from under a bush. One was gray. The other had brown and white spotted markings, a little soft nose, and bright round eyes. He seemed familiar to the Boy.

"Why, he looks like my old Bunny who got lost when I was sick," the Boy thought. He never knew that it really was his own Bunny, returning to look at the Boy who had first helped him to become Real.